FORTUNE'S FOOLS

A ROMEO ROLLER COASTER!

ROSS MONTGOMERY

With illustrations by **Mark Beech**

Barrington Stoke

To all the BFF-4-Evaaaaaaaas

First published in 2023 in Great Britain by
Barrington Stoke Ltd
18 Walker Street, Edinburgh, EH3 7LP

www.barringtonstoke.co.uk

Text © 2023 Ross Montgomery
Illustrations © 2023 Mark Beech

A CIP catalogue record for this book is available
from the British Library upon request

ISBN: 978-1-80090-146-9

Printed by Hussar Books, Poland

CONTENTS

1   Two Households   1

2   Parting is Such Sweet   11
    Sorrow

3   Ready, Steady, Woe!   22

4   They Stumble That Run   31
    Fast

5   You Can't Lose the Game   42
    if You Don't Play the Game

6   Palm to Palm   49

7   Violent Ends   58

CHAPTER 1

Two Households

I sped down the running track as fast as I could. The wind whipped my face and stung my eyes, but nothing could stop me now. My arms were pumping and my heart was racing. I threw myself across the finish line and fell to the track, panting.

"Blake! How did I do?" I asked my best friend, looking up. "Did I beat my fastest time?"

Blake didn't reply. He stood beside the track, playing with his phone as usual. It took

Blake a few seconds to realise I had just asked him a question.

"Huh?" he said. "Oh, sorry, Dom. I didn't know you'd started."

I scowled. "You were supposed to be timing me!"

Blake rolled his eyes. "So?" he said. "You *always* win the hundred metres on Sports Day. You're the best sprinter in school!"

"Well, *you're* best at hurdles!" I replied.

Blake grinned back. "And don't forget, we're both good at ..."

"The relay race!" we said at the same time.

Blake and I were always thinking the same thing at the same time.

Blake pulled me to my feet. "Come on – I'm starving," he said. "Let's go and get some—"

"Lunch!" I said.

"Wow!" gasped Blake. "I was just thinking that!"

"Me too!" I said.

We strolled off to the lunch hall with our arms around each other. It was so lucky that the two best athletes in New Forest Academy were also the two bestest best friends!

Blake and I were the perfect team. We did everything together: training for races, acting in the school drama club, copying each other's homework. We were like two peas in a pod – but if the peas were also really cool and great at sports. All the kids in school called us "D and B" because we were always together!

(Actually, I'd come up with the "D and B" nickname myself and told everyone to use it. I'd also suggested other names: the Supreme Team, the Cool Combo, D-Dog and B-Unit, and the BFF-4-evaaaaaaaaas.)

"Am I still staying at yours tomorrow night?" I asked Blake.

"Of course!" said Blake. "We have to – it's tradition!"

Blake and I always had a sleepover the night before Sports Day so that we could prepare for the big day. Sports Day was the most exciting day of the year. There were four houses in New Forest Academy, all competing to win the House Medal. Parents and teachers cheered from the stands as the whole school was gripped by Sports Day fever.

But things had got a bit out of hand ahead of this year's Sports Day ...

Blake and I walked into the lunch hall. Every single wall was covered in posters, flags, bunting and banners in the different house colours. Some kids were even wearing bracelets and headbands in their house colours. Blake and I grabbed our lunches and sat down, shaking our heads.

"This is ridiculous," said Blake. "Sports Day never used to be like this."

"It's all Mr Fortune's fault," I grumbled. "He never should have changed the house names in the first place!"

Mr Fortune was our head teacher and a huge fan of William Shakespeare. This year he had decided to name all the classes and school buildings after famous Shakespeare plays. Even the food at lunch had a Shakespearean twist: today's options were Cheese and Hamlet sandwiches, the Taming of the Stew and Much Ado About Stuffing. It was all harmless fun ... but then Mr Fortune made a big mistake. He decided to name the school houses after characters from his favourite play, *Romeo and Juliet*.

Romeo and Juliet was about two families, the Montagues and the Capulets, who hated each other. They'd been arguing and fighting in the streets of Verona for years – it seemed like the rivalry would never end! But then one night a young Montague named Romeo met a young Capulet girl named Juliet ... and they both fell head over heels in love. They should have been sworn enemies, but their love was far too strong.

They had a secret wedding, hoping that their marriage would bring their families together. But like all Shakespearean tragedies, it went badly wrong. Romeo's best friend Mercutio was killed in a fight with Juliet's cousin Tybalt. Romeo was so upset he killed Tybalt in revenge. Things went from bad to worse, until Romeo and Juliet tragically lost their lives as well. The Montagues and Capulets were grief-stricken and finally realised how pointless their fighting had been. They put aside their differences once and for all.

Mr Fortune loved the play so much that he decided the four school houses should be named after key characters: Montague House, Capulet

House, Benvolio House and Tybalt House. It was a nice idea, and no one could have expected what happened next ... Montague House and Capulet House really *did* become sworn enemies!

It started off as a joke – kids from different houses teased each other, just like in the play. But soon the jokes became serious. Before long, kids were even insulting each other and starting fights – and then the teachers became involved!

Miss Plant, the drama teacher, was in charge of Montague House, and Mrs Prince, the PE teacher, was in charge of Capulet House. The two teachers had always hated each other, but now they were constantly arguing in the school corridors. It felt like the whole school was divided!

I gazed around the lunch hall. Everywhere you looked, kids with purple Montague headbands were giving mean looks to kids with green Capulet bracelets. I could even see kids bumping each other in the lunch queue. Thank goodness Sports Day was only two days away. By the end of the week, the competition would be over and this silly rivalry would all be forgotten!

"It's kind of funny, isn't it?" I said.

Blake looked blank. "What's funny?" he asked.

"Us two being best mates," I said. "After all, I'm in Montague House and you're in Capulet House. We should be enemies!"

Blake snorted. "What – us two?" he replied. "No way! We're D and B! The Gruesome Twosome!"

"It's Cool Combo," I corrected him. "But you're right – best friends for ever!"

We bumped fists. No matter what happened, Blake and I were always going to be best buddies. Sure, we might end up competing against each other on Sports Day, but no rivalry could *ever* break up our friendship!

Right?

CHAPTER 2

Parting is Such Sweet Sorrow

The next morning, I knew something was wrong the moment I stepped past the school gates.

All of the pupils were huddled together in their different houses, whispering and pointing. All the teachers I passed had faces stiff with shock. Something terrible had happened – but what? I finally found Blake, standing in the playground playing on his phone.

"What's going on?" I asked my best friend. "Why is everyone acting so weird?"

Blake looked up from his phone. "They are?" he said.

I sighed. Blake wasn't very good at paying attention. "Whatever happened, it must be big," I said. "I've never seen everyone look so ..."

Before I could finish my sentence, there were shouts from inside the school.

"This is an outrage!" came a booming voice.

"I demand an explanation!" roared another.

Blake and I shared a glance and then raced into the school to find out what was happening. We peered around the corner of the stairs ... and finally understood what all the fuss was about.

Miss Plant and Mrs Prince were both standing outside Mr Fortune's office, bellowing at the top of their lungs. Miss Plant was holding up the Montague House mascot – a stuffed toy dog giving a thumbs up. Someone had pulled off its ears and bitten its thumb off!

"The Capulets have vandalised Bonio, our beloved mascot!" Miss Plant yelled. Her face had swelled up like a big red balloon. "I demand justice!"

"What about our poster?" Mrs Prince screamed back. She was holding a Capulet House poster covered in graffiti that read "Capulet stinks" and "Montague 4ever". "The Montagues must be punished!" Mrs Prince yelled.

I'd never seen teachers look so angry before. Mr Fortune stood between them, trying to calm them down.

"I-I'm sure there's just been a big misunderstanding," Mr Fortune said gently. "I'll have the mascot repaired and the poster fixed. Now let's try to set a good example for the children, shall we? Can you shake on it?"

Miss Plant and Mrs Prince glared at each other with hate – and shook hands.

"There!" said Mr Fortune. "That's better, isn't it?"

It didn't look like anything was better –
I could hear Miss Plant's and Mrs Prince's
fingers cracking as they "shook hands" from
the end of the corridor. It looked like they
were trying to strangle each other's fingers
to death.

"This is starting to get really silly," I said,
worried.

Blake shrugged. "It's nothing!" he said. "It'll
all be over by lunchtime."

*

But Blake was wrong. I couldn't believe my
eyes when we walked into the lunch hall later.
No one was sitting with their friends – instead,
everyone was sitting with people from their
houses! Montagues sat with Montagues, and
Capulets sat with Capulets. Even the other
houses had picked sides – the Benvolios now
sat with the Montagues, and the Tybalts sat
with the Capulets. All of them were shooting

filthy glances at each other. The tension in the room was horrible – it felt like a fight was about to start any second!

I felt someone grab my arm. It was Steve, the Montague House captain. He gave me a big cheesy grin.

"Dom!" said Steve. "There you are! Come and sit with your housemates!"

I frowned. "Thanks," I said, "but I'm already sitting with Blake ..."

But just then Blake was pulled away by Ruby, the Capulet House captain.

"Oh no he's not!" Ruby cried. "Blake's sitting with us! He's going to *destroy* you stupid Montagues at Sports Day tomorrow!"

"Not if we destroy you first!" shouted Steve.

All the kids at the table started jeering at each other. This was unbelievable. The whole school was turning on each other! Blake and I pulled free and ran out of the lunch hall before the argument could get any worse.

"Now we can't even sit next to each other!" I said. "What do we do?"

Blake shook his head. He was always the most confident out of the two of us. "Forget lunch – we'll grab some snacks on the way home tonight, before the—"

"Sleepover!" I said, brightening up.

Blake gave me a fist bump. "That's right – D and B!"

Blake was right – we didn't need to worry about peer pressure. No one could stop us being best friends!

*

But we got the shock of our lives when Blake and I stepped outside at the end of the day ...

The playground was like a battle site. News of the vandalised poster and mascot must have reached the parents. They were all accusing one another's children and shouting and pointing furious fingers. Mr Fortune was running around, his face as white as a sheet, trying to calm everyone down.

"Er ... now, I'm sure this is all a big misunderstanding ..." he was saying.

And then I saw my mum in the middle of the playground. I ran over.

"Mum?" I asked. "What are you doing here? I'm staying round Blake's tonight, remember?"

But Mum wasn't listening. She was too busy having a screaming match with the man in front of her ... Blake's dad!

"How dare you accuse Dom of damaging that poster?" Mum screamed.

"I didn't accuse him of anything!" roared Blake's dad. "You're just jealous because my Blake is twice the athlete your Dom is!"

Blake and I stared at each other, horrified. Our parents had always got on brilliantly – what was going on?

Mum grabbed my hand, dragging me away. "Come on, Dom," she said, "we're going home!"

I gasped. "But it's the sleepover tonight!"

"The sleepover's cancelled!" Mum shouted. "From now on, you'll have nothing to do with that horrible boy!"

Blake's dad was dragging Blake away too, saying, "Come on, son! We don't need those stuck-up show-offs!"

"Noooooo!" cried Blake. "D-Dog!"

"B-Unit!" I sobbed, reaching out for him. "Come back!"

But it was no use. We couldn't sit next to each other at lunch. We might never be able to go to one another's houses again.

How would our friendship ever survive?

CHAPTER 3

Ready, Steady, Woe!

The next day, things went from bad to worse.
I arrived late for Sports Day because my mum
had car trouble. I raced out of the car and onto
the playing field ... and I couldn't believe what I
was seeing.

All the kids were sitting on the field wearing
their house colours ... but they weren't the
only ones. In the stands, the parents were all
wearing house colours too! There were purple
Montagues, green Capulets, red Benvolios and
yellow Tybalts. Some were even holding up

banners saying "Montague 4ever" or "Capulets rule". New Forest Academy had completely lost the plot!

Steve ran up to me and grabbed my arm. "I've found him, Miss Plant!" Steve cried.

I jumped when I saw Miss Plant. She had painted her face in Montague House colours and looked like a big purple grape.

"Dom!" Miss Plant snapped. "Where have you been? You need to prepare for all your races!"

I blinked, confused. "What do you mean, *all* my races?" I asked.

"You're our best athlete!" Miss Plant said. "You're running in every race."

I felt the colour drain from my face. The races were meant to be shared between all the classes so that every child got the chance to compete. I was going to be exhausted by the end of the day!

"Do I have to?" I begged.

"Of course you do!" said Miss Plant. "Mrs Prince put Blake in every event. There's no way we're letting the Capulets beat us!"

I gasped and looked over at Capulet House. Blake was being shouted at by Mrs Prince. She had *also* painted her face with house colours, so she looked like a big *green* grape. Mrs Prince was clearly in the middle of telling Blake that he had to run in every race, because Blake looked as fed up as I did.

"Dom, please!" begged Steve. "You have to beat Blake! You want us to win the House Medal, don't you?"

All of the other Montagues were urging me to agree. I looked over at the stands and even

my mum was giving me two thumbs up.
I couldn't let them all down, could I?

Mr Fortune stepped into the centre of the playing field, looking nervously at the jeering crowds.

"Er … calm down, please," he said in a weak voice. "The first race is about to begin. Can the competitors for the hurdle dash please proceed to the start line?"

Miss Plant shoved me forwards. "That's you, Dom!" she cried.

"But I'm rubbish at hurdles!" I said.

"Nonsense! You'll do us proud," said Miss Plant. "Death to all Capulets! I mean – good luck, and so on."

The other Montagues almost dragged me to the start line. This was ridiculous. I had to speak to Blake! But when I got to the start line, he was surrounded by a huge crowd of Capulets. They were all shaking their fists at us and calling us "Monta-poo House". The kids from Benvolio House and Tybalt House were joining in too, egging on the rivals. I kept trying to catch Blake's eye, but I couldn't get anywhere near him!

"Competitors ready!" announced Mr Fortune.

It was too late to talk to Blake. I turned to face the race track. It was lined with Montagues and Benvolios on one side, and Capulets and Tybalts on the other. The hurdle dash was my worst race ... but I couldn't turn back now. I crouched down, took a deep breath and waited for Mr Fortune to fire the starting pistol ...

BANG!

I shot from the start line as fast as I could, leaping into the air. I cleared the first hurdle with ease. Most of the other competitors fell behind quickly – but I could just see Blake in the corner of my eye. We were neck and neck!

The crowd were a blur as I zoomed past, deafening me with their shouts and screams. Another hurdle ... then another, and another. Now only one was left between me and the finish line. Blake and I were still tied in first place. The final hurdle came up ...

I jumped too late. My foot caught on the hurdle. I fell to the ground, bashing my knee painfully on the track and knocking all the breath out of me. There was a huge roar from the Capulets as Blake flew over the finish line to take first place. I lay on the ground, the world spinning as a big gang of Montagues stood over me.

"Dom!" cried Steve. "Are you OK?"

"It's just a scratch," I said, glancing at my bleeding knee. "Maybe I should sit out the next race to rest my leg."

"Oh no you don't!" cried Miss Plant. "Blake's in the next race too, and you're the only one who can beat him!"

This was getting annoying now. "Where *is* Blake?" I asked.

I glanced around, looking for him. I couldn't see Blake anywhere. Normally, he'd be helping me to my feet and checking I was OK ...

Then I saw him. Blake was standing at the finish line, surrounded by cheering Capulets. They were patting his back and lifting him onto their shoulders. Blake looked ... well, he looked *delighted*. He didn't care that I was hurt – he hadn't even noticed. The other Capulets were pointing and laughing at me as I lay bleeding on the ground.

And suddenly I saw red. Blake was supposed to be my best friend in the whole world, but all he seemed to care about was winning the race. Was that all my friendship meant to him? What had happened to D and B – the Cool Combo? The BFF-4-evaaaaaaaas?

I gritted my teeth and pushed myself to my feet.

"Forget resting my leg," I said. "Take me to the next race. From now on, it's not Sports Day. It's war!"

CHAPTER 4

They Stumble That Run Fast

I limped to the start line for the next race, the cut on my knee making me wince. Blake strolled over to join me, grinning like a Cheshire cat.

"Great race, Dom," he said sarcastically.

I turned away angrily. How could Blake be so cruel? I thought we were best friends!

But I wasn't going to let Blake get to me. I wasn't even going to speak to him. Out of the corner of my eye, I saw Blake's cocky smile disappear.

That's right, Blake, I thought. *It's the hundred-metre sprint – my best race. Get ready to eat my dust!*

The other competitors joined us and the race began. Blake and I started off neck and neck again – but even with my injured knee, there was no beating me! I shot across the finish line and knew from the roar of triumph from Montague House that I had won. I turned around and saw Blake leaning over his knees, panting. I strode past him, not even bothering to shake his hand.

"See you at the next race!" I called cattily backwards.

The rest of the day was a blur. Blake and I ran race after race, one after the other. Normally, I'd have been exhausted after just a few. But I was so angry with Blake that I hardly noticed how tired I was. I couldn't even feel the pain in my knee any more – I was too determined to beat him!

It wasn't just races we competed in. Blake and I were made to take part in field events too. The tug of war, the shot-put, the obstacle course, the long jump. Each time, it was always me or Blake who won. For every race that I won, Blake won the next. We were perfectly matched: Benvolio House and Tybalt House didn't stand a chance!

The points stacked up one by one: first Montague House was in the lead, then Capulet House, then Montague again, then Capulet once more.

As the day went on, the atmosphere on the playing field became stranger and stranger. The kids watching had nothing to do but sit in the sun all day and watch me and Blake compete, and they grew hot and agitated. They began shouting insults and starting fights with each other. Everyone was behaving like complete fools!

The parents were just as bad. Every time a race finished, the parents in the stands began arguing, accusing me or Blake of cheating. Soon they were even jumping out of the stands and storming over to Mr Fortune, demanding that races be repeated!

Mr Fortune was in way over his head. At first he tried to calm down the parents by referring to the Sports Day rulebook, pointing out that no one had cheated ... But before long, the parents became too angry to reason with. Mr Fortune had to barricade himself inside the games shed on the other side of the field for his own safety. He held a javelin for protection out of the window and announced the races with a megaphone!

"TWO – RACES – LEFT!" Mr Fortune cried, sounding miserable. "The house relay race, followed by the three-legged race. Competitors in your places, please!"

I gasped. The three-legged race was a silly race to finish the day – anyone could take part, and it was supposed to be a fun finale to the day. But the house relay was the most important race of Sports Day. It was the only race where the winning house got double points – and Montague House and Capulet House were in joint first place. That meant whoever came first would win Sports Day!

There were four runners in the race from each house. I would be the last of the Montague runners – Blake would be the last of the Capulets. Once again, I'd be running against my old best friend ... only now, he was my worst enemy.

I didn't even look at Blake as I took my position on the track. We were both equally good at the relay race. All I knew was I had to get over the finish line before he did. That would wipe the annoying smirk off his face once and for all!

Mr Fortune fired the starting pistol from the games-shed window, but I could hardly hear it over the roar of the crowd. The first runners flew from the start line, running once around the track before passing the baton to the next racers.

The Benvolio and Tybalt House teams quickly fell behind. Once again, it was between Montague House and Capulet House. The baton was soon passed on to the next runners – Steve and Ruby – who sped towards me and Blake.

I prepared myself, trembling with anticipation. I glanced over at Blake, who shot me a filthy look. I had to run like I'd never run before!

Steve passed me the baton just as Ruby passed hers to Blake. We charged ahead at exactly the same time, our eyes fixed on the finishing line. I gave everything I had, my arms pumping and every muscle burning in my body. But I couldn't help myself – I kept looking over at Blake to see if he was beating me. And he was doing the same to me! We glared at each other with rage as we sprinted onwards ...

And then it all went wrong. We both tripped at the exact same time. We flew through the air at the same time. Blake and I crashed into each other, letting out identical howls of pain ... Then we both hit the ground like two sacks of spuds in perfect unison.

I felt the shooting pain right away. I knew
that I had twisted my ankle, and badly too.
Beside me, Blake was screaming with agony,
clutching his leg as well. We hadn't managed
to cross the finish line – we were just a few
centimetres away from it. Before I could even
think about getting up, Taylor from Tybalt

House flew past us and crossed the finish line. The house relay hadn't been won by either of us!

Within seconds, Blake and I were surrounded by a crowd of children. Miss Plant and Mrs Prince pushed themselves to the front.

"You dirty cheats!" Miss Plant shouted at Mrs Prince. "Blake tripped up my Dom!"

"Oh no he didn't!" cried Mrs Prince. "It was all Dom's fault! I *demand* a re-run!"

Mr Fortune's voice came out of the megaphone from the games shed on the other side of the field.

"There will be no repeat of the house relay!" he cried. "It was won by Tybalt House, fair and square!"

Everyone looked up at the leader board. The points from the house relay were being added to Tybalt House, but they were still miles behind first place. Benvolio House hadn't won a single race. Montague House and Capulet House were still tied in the lead.

"Now, everyone, please prepare for the three-legged race," Mr Fortune said. "Then we can all go home and maybe have a good cry."

Everyone stared at each other. We all worked it out at the same time. The three-legged race was the final race of the day. Whoever won it would win the House Medal!

"Dom, get up!" cried Miss Plant. "We need you!"

But there was no way I could take part. My leg felt like it was filled with red-hot needles!

"Ha ha ha!" said Ruby, pointing at me as I lay on the ground. "You Montagues are stuffed – you've lost your best athlete!"

"So have you!" snapped Steve.

He pointed at Blake, who looked like he was in just as much pain as me. One thing was certain: Blake and I had crashed out of Sports Day.

"Can someone help me up, please …?" I begged.

But no one even noticed I had spoken. Everyone was too busy preparing for the next race, deciding who their best competitors were now that Blake and I were out. They all ran away, arguing at the top of their lungs. Blake and I were left sprawled on the track like broken, forgotten toys. They didn't care that we were hurt. All they cared about was winning the House Medal!

My eyes filled with tears. I had lost the race … and I had lost the support of Montague House too.

But most importantly of all, I had lost my best friend.

CHAPTER 5

You Can't Lose the Game if You Don't Play the Game

A few minutes later, Blake and I limped into the school nurse's office together. Neither of us wanted to be near each other, but there was nothing we could do about it. The nurse took one look at us and sighed.

"Another Sports Day injury!" she said. "Anything broken?"

"Just my heart," I whispered, and I shot Blake a hurt look.

"You can talk!" snapped Blake. "You made me fall over!"

"*You* made *me* fall over!" I spluttered.

The nurse rolled her eyes. She made Blake and I sit next to each other on the bed as she checked my leg.

"Nothing serious," the nurse said. "It looks like you've twisted your right ankle." She checked Blake's leg. "And *you've* twisted your left ankle. Talk about two peas in a pod!"

Blake and I stared at the floor in silence. There was a time when we'd probably have been happy to have the same injury – but not any more. Now it just reminded us of the friendship we had lost.

The nurse left the office to get some bandages. Blake and I were left alone to glare at each other.

"After today, I never want to see you again," Blake hissed.

"Fine by me!" I cried. "I don't see how you can act all hurt when you left me lying injured after the hurdles. I thought we were friends!"

Blake looked shocked. "You were injured in the hurdles?" he asked.

"You knew I was!" I shouted. "And you didn't even come to help me!"

Blake shook his head. "I really didn't know!" he said. "When the race was over, everyone ran up and stood around me. It was really confusing. I couldn't see you anywhere!"

I frowned. That made sense – I was lying on the ground, surrounded by Montagues. "Well, what about what you said at the beginning of the next race?" I said. "You didn't have to be so sarcastic to me!"

"Sarcastic?" said Blake, looking blank. "I wasn't being sarcastic. I really was wishing you good luck!"

That made sense too. Blake was never sarcastic. I wasn't sure he even knew *how* to be sarcastic.

"I wondered why you turned away when I said it," said Blake, sounding hurt. "I couldn't understand why you were being so competitive with me all day!"

The truth was beginning to dawn on me. Blake and I had been complete fools. We each thought that the other was being a bad friend. We had totally misunderstood each other.

"I didn't realise," I said.

"Me neither," said Blake. "I'm ..."

"Sorry," we both said at the same time.

We fell silent, both ashamed. The only
sound was the mob of parents and teachers
and children on the playing field. They were
all shouting while Mr Fortune begged them
over the megaphone to be sensible.

"Listen to them," I said. "When that
three-legged race starts, it's going to be
carnage no matter who wins!"

"Maybe they'll burn the school down," said Blake, cheering up. "That could be OK."

I shook my head. "Maybe we can talk some sense into them before it's too late ..." I said.

I tried to step off the bed – but the moment I put my right ankle on the floor, I felt a shooting stab of pain up my leg. I had to lean on Blake for support. At that moment, the nurse came in with a handful of bandages and glared at me.

"Where do you think *you're* going?" she said.

"We have to get to the playing field," I cried. "It's important!"

"Oh – no – you – don't!" the nurse said. "If you think you're doing any more races with a twisted ankle, you've got another think coming! The only way you two are getting out of here is if you're leaning on each other!"

I looked at Blake. Blake looked at me. As usual, we'd just had the exact same idea at the same time.

"Leaning on each other, you say ...?" I replied with a smile.

CHAPTER 6

Palm to Palm

Back at the playing field, Sports Day had
gone from bad to worse to *even* worse. The
three-legged race was *supposed* to be fun ... but
there was nothing fun about it now. Montague
House and Capulet House were trying to enter
every single child they could so that they had
a better chance of winning. The start line was
clogged with children tied at the ankles. The air
was filled with shouts and cries and the sounds
of children falling over.

"That's not fair!" Mrs Prince cried. "Montague House has entered more people than us!"

"So?!" said Miss Plant. "The Sports Day rulebook says that there's no maximum number of competitors for the three-legged race! Isn't that right, Mr Fortune?"

Mr Fortune was leaning out of the window of the games shed with the rulebook.

"That's correct," he whimpered. "Each house may enter as many children as they wish ..."

But then a hush seemed to fall over the crowd. Everyone stopped what they were doing and turned to face what was heading across the playing field towards them. The parents stopped arguing in the stands, and the kids fell silent.

It was me and Blake. We were leaning on each other for support, with our arms over the other's shoulders. We had tied our twisted ankles together with a set of bandages and were limping steadily towards the start line.

"Dom!" said Miss Plant. "What on earth are you doing?"

"What do you think?" I said. "We're getting ready for the three-legged race!"

"You and ... Blake?" Mrs Prince spluttered with outrage. "Out of the question! Untie yourselves at once and pick someone from your own house to partner with!"

"That's correct!" cried Miss Plant, agreeing with Mrs Prince for the first time. "It's against the rules! You have to pair up with someone from your own house!"

"Oh no they don't!" shouted Mr Fortune.

Everyone turned around. Mr Fortune was waving the rulebook out of the games-shed window.

"The three-legged race is a fun run," he yelled. "That means people can partner with whoever they want. There's nothing in the rulebook that says you have to run with someone in your own house!"

Miss Plant and Mrs Prince were somehow turning ghost white and bright red at the same time.

"But Montague House and Capulet House are both tied for first place!" said Miss Plant. "If Dom and Blake win the race ..."

"It'll still be a tie!" finished Mrs Prince. "No one will win!"

By now everyone on the playing field was whispering in disbelief. Steve ran up to me and tried to drag me away.

"Don't do it, Dom!" he begged. "Run with me – we can win for Montague House!"

Ruby ran up to Blake and tried to pull him away too. "Run with me, Blake! You can't let the Capulets lose when we're so close to winning!"

But it was no use. They couldn't pull me and Blake apart. We had our hands clamped over each other's shoulders and our ankles tied together. We were like two peas in a pod.

"We're running together, and that's that," I said. "D and B!"

"The Cruddy Buddies!" said Blake, fist-bumping me.

"It's Cool Combo," I corrected him. I turned to Steve. "Now if you don't mind, we have a race to win."

We got ready at the start line. Ruby and Steve stared at us, shocked.

"They've lost the plot!" Steve shrieked.

"Fools! They're both fools!" cried Ruby.

"Montagues, on your marks!" wailed Miss Plant.

"Don't let them win, Capulets!" bellowed Mrs Prince.

Everyone crammed together at the start line, bustling and shoving to try to get the best spot. It was chaos. Everyone was so determined to get a good position that no one seemed to notice when Mr Fortune fired the starting pistol!

But Blake and I did – we charged ahead, perfectly in time, and steamed towards the finish line. Our ankles were still injured, but now that they were tied together, we were stronger than ever. One, two, three, four … step by step, we hopped past the screaming parents who now lined the track, ignoring all of them.

"Dom!" cried my mum. "What are you doing?"

"Blake! Stop it!" cried Blake's dad.

But we didn't stop. The competition didn't stand a chance. None of the other children were working together. They were just trying to run as fast as they could, then falling out of rhythm and getting their ankles tangled. Ruby and Claire kept crashing into each other. Steve was charging after us as fast as he could, dragging a screaming Leo along the ground behind him.

"Stop them!" cried Miss Plant. "Don't let them win …!"

But they couldn't stop us. Blake and I had our arms around each other and a massive grin on our faces as we flew over the finish line together. We had done it – the House Medal had been won by Montague House *and* Capulet House!

That summed up me and Blake perfectly. We had always finished each other's sentences. Now we were even finishing each other's races too.

CHAPTER 7

Violent Ends

The playing field was totally silent for a moment. Normally, the air would be filled with cheering and whooping and celebrating after the three-legged race. Instead, every single child and teacher and parent was staring at us, their mouths open with horror.

"They both won!" cried Miss Plant. "It's … a tie!"

"It … it's not over!" shouted Mrs Prince. "We can do the race again."

"Ha! You Capulets would like that, wouldn't you?" sneered Steve. "You'll just use it as a chance to cheat!"

"Us?! Cheat?" cried Ruby. "You Montagues have been cheating all day!"

"That's right!" said Blake's dad, turning to face my mum. "Your son cheated!"

"He did not!" growled my mum. "Dom was practically carrying your useless lump of a son to the finish line!"

"My son is no LUMP!" screamed Blake's dad.

Within seconds, the playing field was like a battlefield. Teachers fought, children shouted, parents accused each other of doing their children's homework for them and stealing lost property. All Blake and I could do was watch in shock. What had we done? There was no way anyone could stop this mob!

At this rate, the school really was going to be burned to the ground ...

"STOP!" cried a loud voice.

Everyone stopped what they were doing and turned to the games shed. Mr Fortune was standing on the roof, wearing his vest, holding the megaphone in one hand. In the other hand he was waving a white flag made from a javelin with his shirt tied at the end.

Finally, after a long and tiring day, Mr Fortune had had enough.

"What is *wrong* with all of you?" he cried. "Look at yourselves! All this fighting, all this arguing ... for what? Sports Day is supposed to be *fun!*"

Everyone looked at each other. It was true – it had been a miserable day. Mr Fortune pointed at me and Blake.

"Look at these two!" he said. "They're in different houses. They *should* be rivals … but instead, they've raced together. They've supported each other. Dom and Blake put aside their differences and celebrated their friendship … If they can, surely *everyone* can?"

The mob looked at their feet shamefully. No one said anything for a moment. Then an amazing thing happened. Steve turned to Ruby and held out his hand.

"Er … sorry for all the things I said today," Steve muttered. "Your house raced really well."

Ruby smiled and shook his hand. "Sorry for everything *I* said, too. And sorry for putting frogs in your locker earlier."

Steve's eyes widened. "You did what?" he said.

But now everyone was making up. All the friends who had fallen out were finding each other and hugging. In the stands, parents were blushing with embarrassment and muttering apologies, making plans to meet up the following week. I looked over at Mum – I was relieved to see she was apologising to Blake's dad.

"I'm so sorry," said Mum. "I don't know what came over me. Your son did brilliantly today."

"So did yours!" said Blake's dad. "I'm really glad he and Blake are such good friends."

Blake and I stared at each other, hardly able to believe it. Had we *really* done all this? Could this day get any stranger?

But then the strangest thing of all happened. Miss Plant pushed her way through the crowd to stand in front of Mrs Prince. The two sworn enemies faced each other: one painted purple, one painted green. They didn't say a word for a moment ... and then they threw themselves into each other's arms, sobbing with emotion.

"Oh, Daisy!" wailed Miss Plant to Mrs Prince. "What have we done? We never should have fallen out over that silly school baking competition ..."

"No, it was my fault, Barbara!" sobbed Mrs Prince to Miss Plant. "I shouldn't have been so rude about your muffins!"

"Well, *I* insulted your Battenberg!" said Miss Plant.

Mrs Prince wiped away a tear. "We've been such fools!" she said. "We were best friends once ... could we be best friends again?"

"Of course!" said Mrs Prince. "We were always like two peas in ..."

"A pod!" finished Miss Plant, giving Mrs Prince a high five. "D and B!"

I was absolutely speechless. Miss Plant and Mrs Prince had once been best friends. They even had the same initials as us!

Steve clapped a hand on my shoulder. "What are you both waiting for?" he said. "Get on that podium and take the House Medal!"

I frowned. "But the house captains are supposed to accept the medal," I said.

Ruby snorted. "Forget that," she said. "You two are the only winners here!"

Blake and I grinned. We limped over to the podium arm in arm, our ankles still tied together, and stepped onto the first-place block. Rianna from Tybalt House stood in second place and Beth from Benvolio House stood in third place. Mr Fortune climbed down from the games-shed roof and strolled over with the medals, grinning with relief. He looked at us and then looked at the medals, confused.

"Oh, bother," Mr Fortune said. "This has never happened before – I've only got the one gold medal. You two don't mind sharing, do you?"

"Of course we don't!" I said.

"But how are we going to fit the medal around both our necks?" asked Blake.

The idea came to me in a heartbeat. I untied the bandages from around our ankles, undid the medal's ribbon and tied the bandages to each end. Now it was the perfect size for two!

I hung the gold medal around our necks, and the whole playing field cheered. I felt amazing. Here I was, winning the House Medal for Montague House ... and I was doing it with my best friend in the whole wide world.

I turned to face Blake – my bezzie, my bro – and pulled him in for a hug.

"Great race, Blake!" I said.

"Great race, Dom!" said Blake.

It was the perfect ending to the day. Montague House and Capulet House might have both won Sports Day … but the *real* winner was friendship.

Our books are tested
for children and young people by
children and young people.

Thanks to everyone who consulted on
a manuscript for their time and effort in
helping us to make our books better
for our readers.